Christmas Surprise

Words by Hilary Robinson

www.hilaryrobinson.co.uk

Pictures by Mandy Stanley

www.mandystanley.com

STRAUSS HOUSE PRODUCTIONS

Lumby Grange, Lumby, South Milford, North Yorkshire, LS25 5JA

www.thecoppertree.org

First published in Great Britain 2012

Text copyright © Hilary Robinson 2012

Illustrations copyright © Mandy Stanley 2012

Hilary Robinson and Mandy Stanley have asserted their rights
to be identified as the author and illustrator of this work under
The Copyright, Designs and Patents Act, 1988

British Library Cataloguing in Publication Data

A catalogue record for this book is available from the British Library

All rights reserved. ISBN 978-0-9571245-1-6

Printed in the UK

Christmas Surprise

For Hal
HR

For Alfie Tiger
MS

Hilary Robinson & Mandy Stanley

STRAUSS HOUSE
PRODUCTIONS

A few days ago Rupal's mum came to school. She asked Mr Banks if Copper Tree class could visit the elderly people at the Pine Lodge Care Home where she works with Rupal's dad.

Rupal's mum brought two pets with her.

Bobby and Bess used to pull heavy sledges before
they retired. They now live a quieter life at Pine Lodge.

Bonnie

She said that another pet, a retired guide dog called Bonnie, had been at the animal hospital for a few days and everyone was missing her. Bonnie used to help people who can't see. She thought a visit from Copper Tree class would really cheer them up.

Mr Banks asked us if we had any ideas about what we could do.

I said we could sing a few songs like Little Donkey which we did in our Christmas play when I played the triangle. The only thing was when we did the clip-clop sounds with coconut shells, Alfie Tate got a bit excited and the Little Donkey sounded like it was galloping and we started singing faster and faster and we all got mixed up.

Mr Banks said he was sure we could sort that out and we could sing We Wish You A Merry Christmas as well because everyone knows the words.

Rupal said that a lady called Violet Starr would like that because she doesn't always remember things but she does remember the words to songs because she used to be a singer.

Jake said we could help to decorate their lounge.

He likes growing things and brought in holly and ivy and bags of fir cones which we'd painted and used to decorate our classroom.

Rupal said that Mr Potts, who is ninety years old, would like Jake's idea because he used to be a gardener at a big house.

Mr Potts told her that they always put up the biggest Christmas tree in the world and they needed scaffolding to get to the top.

He said they put some chocolate coins on it that got nibbled by mice!
Alfie Tate said, 'They should have put cheese on the tree too!'

Holly doesn't say very much but
Mr Banks asked her for some ideas.

Alfie

Me (Olivia)

Hana and Barnie

Rupal

Jake

Erika

Holly

She whispered that she'd like us all to dress up like we did when we were in Willow Tree class and she was an angel.

Mr Banks said dressing up would be a good idea and we could also decorate the lounge at Pine Lodge.

Alfie Tate said if we sang Little Donkey he would bring a real donkey from the Donkey Sanctuary. He said they used to give rides at seasides before they retired.

Lots of people stopped to watch us walk up the high street. Mr Banks said, 'Well it's not every day we see Alfie Tate dressed as a robin.' Alfie kept holding us up because he stopped every time he saw a real one.

Rupal's mum showed us round the home. All the rooms had photos on the doors of the elderly people and Bonnie, Bobby and Bess in their younger days.

She explained that she wanted carers and visitors to understand
a little bit about the residents' lives before they came to live there.

Mr Potts helped us to decorate the lounge and the Christmas tree.

He told us stories about the mice in the big house and how he thought they liked to party in the Grand Hall when everyone had gone to bed.

Then we sang We Wish You A Merry Christmas and Violet Starr sang louder than all of us put together!

At the end, Rupal's Mum said that they had a surprise for us.
Bonnie was much better and because it was now snowing
Bobby and Bess had brought her...

...home in time for Christmas!

Copper Tree Class

Help A Hamster

Book Three!

It was a squeeze in the hamster house after Henry had four baby hamsters.
Alfie Tate was the emergency hamster monitor because our teacher said he would
be the 'Best person for the job!' That's because Alfie was adopted by his mum and
dad and he told us all about it. We found homes for three hamsters but
no one wanted the smallest.

Find out what happens in book three of the Copper Tree series,
Copper Tree Class Help A Hamster.

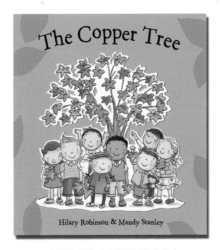

ISBN 978-0-9571245-0-9

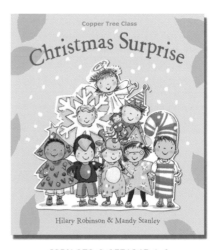

ISBN 978-0-9571245-1-6

www.strausshouseproductions.com

www.thecoppertree.org

STRAUSS HOUSE
PRODUCTIONS